5/18

Big, Brave, Bold
SERGIO

To my Dad, who listened over and over to this story in the works, but missed hearing the final manuscript—DW

For my sister, Jessica—JT

Published by
MAGINATION PRESS®
American Psychological Association
750 First Street NE
Washington, DC 20002

Magination Press is a registered trademark of the American Psychological Association.

For more information about our books, including a complete catalog, please write to us, call 1-800-374-2721, or visit our website at www.apa.org/pubs/magination.

Book design by Gwen Grafft

Printed by Lake Book Manufacturing, Inc., Melrose Park, IL

Library of Congress Cataloging-in-Publication Data

Names: Wagenbach, Debbie, author. | Tablason, Jamie, illustrator.
Title: Big brave bold Sergio / by Debbie Wagenbach ; illustrated by
  Jamie Tablason.
Description: Washington, DC : Magination Press, American Psychological
  Association, [2018] | Summary: When little Sergio realizes that the
  Snapper gang bullies others, he breaks away from them and makes
  friends, only to become the new target of the gang's bullying.
Identifiers: LCCN 2017023282 | ISBN 9781433827945 (hardcover) | :
  1433827948 (hardcover)
Subjects: | CYAC: Conduct of life—Fiction. | Gangs—Fiction. |
  Bullying—Fiction. | Friendship—Fiction. | Turtles—Fiction.
Classification: LCC PZ7.W1216 Big 2018 | DDC [E]—dc23 LC
  record available at https://lccn.loc.gov/2017023282

Manufactured in the United States of America
10 9 8 7 6 5 4 3 2 1

Big, Brave, Bold
SERGIO

by Debbie Wagenbach
illustrated by Jamie Tablason

Magination Press • Washington, DC • American Psychological Association

Sergio liked swimming with the Snappers.

He felt **BIG** when they scattered the minnows.

He felt **BRAVE** when they played soccer with the snails.

He felt **BOLD** when they plucked tail feathers from the ducks.

Lately, though, Sergio noticed how others quivered when the Snappers swam by. This bothered him, but when he mentioned it to one of the other Snappers, Big Clay nipped at him.

"Don't let any squishy feelings stick to your shell, Sergio. You are a Snapper and Snappers hate squishy feelings. Squishy feelings will make you soft and weak!" Sergio did not argue, but he wondered more and more if this was where he fit in.

One day the Snappers picked on a tiny fish named Gil. "Let's have some fun with this morsel of pond scum! He's not even big enough to taste!" snapped Big Clay. He snatched Gil's glasses and flipper-flung them to another Snapper.

Gil zipped.

Gil zigged.

Gil zagged.

But he could not
grab his glasses.

"Bury them, Sergio!"
demanded Big Clay.

Sergio turned to dive and came face to face with Gil.
At that moment, Sergio did not feel big, brave, or bold.
He felt small and squishy. Maybe he *was* getting soft.
He tossed Gil his glasses and let him swim away.

The Snappers glared at Sergio. They called
him names. They flicked sand in his face.
They threatened to kick him out of the group.

Sergio tried to fit in, but he just didn't. He buried his belly in the sand and sank into his shell.

The next morning, Sergio felt a tap, tap, tapping on his shell.

It was Gil. "My friends and I are playing hide
and seek," he whispered. "Would you like to play?"

Sergio sighed. "Me?"

"Yes, you," bubbled Gil.

Sergio dug out of the sand and swam off to play.
Soon he had many new friends.

He quacked with the ducks, snoozed with the snails…

...and blushed when the minnows blew him kisses.

The Snappers fumed. They hatched a plan.

One day, they shoved him in the sand,
tangled him in seaweed, and snapped at his tail.
"That's what you get!" they hissed.

Sergio untangled himself and pulled inside an old log.

At dusk, a commotion stirred the water. Sergio peeked out. Across the pond, Big Clay battled a hook and line. He twisted. He turned. He could not break free.

That's what HE gets, thought Sergio.
But as he watched, Sergio had that squishy
feeling again. Big Clay needed help.

With a shout, Sergio whooshed
through the pond. Water splashed
and bubbles churned as he leaped
and snapped the fishing line in two.

Big Clay dropped into the pond
as the rest of the Snappers stared.

"I had it under control," Big Clay said. "But that was cool. Do you want to come back and swim with the gang?"

"No thanks," Sergio said. "Let's just all be friends."

Gil sped over to Sergio. They gave each other fin-to-flipper high-fives as all his friends cheered for **BIG, BRAVE, BOLD SERGIO**!

NOTE TO PARENTS AND CAREGIVERS

Julia Martin Burch, PhD

Learning to develop and navigate friendships is a fun, challenging, and critical part of child and adolescent development. Through friendships, children learn the building blocks of how to start and maintain a relationship with another person, an important skill they will use throughout their lives. They also learn related skills like sharing, resolving arguments, and compromising. And of course, friendships are fun! Being liked and accepted by peers makes children feel good—in fact, it can often feel like the most important thing in their world. With these powerful, exciting, and enjoyable relationships, however, come challenges, particularly learning to cope with peer pressure and to differentiate one's own sense of right and wrong from that of one's peer group. You may vividly remember struggling with such challenges yourself as a child.

How This Book Can Help

Just as Sergio experiences in the story, standing up for kindness and compassion in the face of peer pressure is one of the more difficult challenges children and adolescents face. As you talk through it, help your child think through the various characters' perspectives. For example, you might ask "how do you think Gil felt when the Snappers were being mean?" "Why do you think Sergio saved Big Clay even though he was mad at him?" Helping your child learn to take other's perspectives and consider how to solve a problem from multiple viewpoints is a critical component to developing empathy.

What You Can Do

As parents, caretakers, and teachers, you are in a unique position to help the children in your care develop healthy, fulfilling friendships and cultivate a sense of empathy and right and wrong. You also have the important job of making sure your children understand what peer pressure and bullying are, and know how to deal with these challenges and when to seek adult help.

Nurture your child's developing empathy. Throughout childhood and adolescence, children develop an increasingly sophisticated understanding of right and wrong. During infancy and toddlerhood, children are predominantly focused on themselves and getting their own way. But by late preschool and grade school, they begin to understand the Golden Rule (act towards others as you want them to act towards you), as well as behavioral norms, values, and moral lessons from their environment (e.g., "It is wrong to steal from the store," or "I should be kind to others").

Unlike physical development, which occurs with or without adult help, a child's moral development requires your guidance and support. Some of that guidance occurs naturally. For example, children learn by watching you, so model the type of empathic or values-driven behavior you want to see from your children. If you are dealing with a moral dilemma that is child-appropriate, you can consider discussing your own thinking and problem-solving with your child. For example, if a store cashier accidentally put some items in your bag without charging you, gently bring this to their attention in front of your child and, later, discuss the importance of honesty with your child. You can also engage your child in discussion about morally ambiguous or challenging social situations from books and television shows. Entertainment depicting conflicts between children is a particularly rich opportunity to help your child proactively think about how she might resolve a similar situation in a way that she would feel proud of later.

Make room for "squishy" feelings.
Learning to listen to one's gut or to those "squishy feelings" is a key factor in developing a sense of right and wrong. Those squishy feelings tell us when something is not right, so encourage your child to notice and pay attention when he has his own squishy feelings in a social situation. Talk to him about what was going on and help him figure out how he might want to act next time. For example, you might say "it sounds like you were feeling upset because your classmates were not being nice to the new kid and you were not sure what to do about it. I am so glad you paid attention to that feeling because it's important to be kind, especially if other kids are being mean. Maybe you can invite the new student to sit with you at lunch tomorrow." Additionally, praise your child for noticing his feelings. Never make fun of your child for being sensitive about a difficult social situation. Part of raising an empathic, compassionate child is showing the same compassion for his feelings.

Help kids cope with peer pressure and bullying. Humans are social animals; we like to belong to a group and feel as though we fit in, and children are no different. In fact, research suggests that a sense of belonging is a key factor contributing to a child's happiness, mental health, and general well-being. Trouble can arise, however, when a child's friends act in ways that oppose her own values.

While it is normal for other kids to have different values, opinions, preferences, and material things, it is never okay to tease or make fun of a child for being different.

Encourage your child to always

tell you or another trusted adult if they witness or are a victim of teasing or bullying.

Emphasize that adult intervention is often necessary to put an end to a harmful situation. Coach your child in how to respond to mild peer pressure or teasing. Calmly and firmly stating "I'm not comfortable with that" or "I need to think about that" allows a child to set boundaries with a peer without exacerbating the situation as yelling, crying, or tattling might. When your child shares an experience of mild peer pressure or teasing, resist the urge to immediately call the school or the other child's parents (as long as the situation does not require immediate adult intervention). Instead, help your child think through how he might respond to such pressure in the future. For example, if a child is being teased about his backpack, he might practice responding "I like my backpack. It's really comfortable and can fit a lot of Legos in it!" Practicing these responses with you in a calm situation better enables your child to stand up for himself or others in real time with peers. It can also allow children to calmly extricate themselves from a situation that they need to alert an adult to.

Prevent bullying behavior. If you suspect your child might be teasing or bullying others, have an open and calm conversation with her about it. Ask her what happened, and avoid criticizing. Help her take the other child's perspective by asking questions about how she thinks the other child might feel and if she would want someone to treat her that way. Discuss your family's or community's values ("we are kind to others in this family, so we do not behave in that way"). Calmly share the consequences for her behavior and be sure to follow through. While losing a privilege such as screen time is often an effective consequence, consider having your child write a reflection on how she will treat others differently in the future or how the bullying might have hurt the other child's feelings. This kind of consequence promotes new learning and empathy in addition to punishing the bullying behavior. You can also help your child think through and role play ways to communicate to her peer group that she is no longer going to engage in bullying behavior. Also encourage her to play with lots of different children. As Sergio discovers, it is just as fun to quack with the ducks and snooze with the snails as it is to swim with the Snappers!

Finally, help your child find prosocial ways to feel big, brave, and bold. Create opportunities for him to help others, such as doing a community service project or volunteering together as a family. Coach him to befriend and stand up for kids who are teased. You can use Sergio's story to talk through the importance of doing what's right, even when it is hard or when you are angry, such as when Sergio freed Big Clay from the fishing line.

It is important to note that bullying leads to long-lasting negative consequences for children. Research has found that the longer a child is engaging in bullying or is being bullied, the worse the consequence. Thus, if you suspect your child is a bully or is being bullied, it is very important to intervene early through the school and at home. Also consider taking your child to see a mental health professional who specializes in children.

Julia Martin Burch, PhD, is a postdoctoral fellow in child and adolescent psychology at McLean Hospital. Dr. Martin Burch completed her training at Fairleigh Dickinson University and Massachusetts General Hospital/Harvard Medical School. She works with children, teens, and parents, and specializes in cognitive behavioral therapy for anxiety, obsessive compulsive, and related disorders.

ABOUT THE AUTHOR

Debbie Wagenbach grew up on a farm in southeast Iowa, the oldest of nine siblings. She has been reading and telling stories to children for as long as she can remember. As a retired children's librarian, she now writes books for children herself, mostly during the daylight hours. Debbie still lives on the same farm, where she enjoys quiet strolls on dusty roads, cloud watching, savoring a daily smidge of dark chocolate, and introducing her great nieces and nephews to the loveliest of books.

ABOUT THE ILLUSTRATOR

Jamie Tablason loves illustrating for children and the young at heart. Through whimsical imagery and engaging characters, she hopes to connect with her audience and inspire young and old to tell their own stories. Jamie received her BFA and MA in illustration from CSU Long Beach, School of Art. She currently works and lives in Lakewood, CA, with her husband and their two dogs, a basset hound and bulldog.

ABOUT MAGINATION PRESS

Magination Press is an imprint of the American Psychological Association, the largest scientific and professional organization representing psychologists in the United States and the largest association of psychologists worldwide.